SUPER SPORTS STAR

DAUNTE CULPEPPER

Stew Thornley

Enslow Publishers, Inc.

40 Industrial Road   PO Box 38
Box 398   Aldershot
Berkeley Heights, NJ 07922 Hants GU12 6BP
USA   UK

http://www.enslow.com

Library of Congress Cataloging-in-Publication Data

Thornley, Stew.
   Super sports star Daunte Culpepper / Stew Thornley.
      p. cm. — (Super sports star)
   Summary: A biography of the star quarterback for the Minnesota Vikings.
   Includes bibliographical references (p.   ) and index.
   ISBN 0-7660-2051-7
   1. Culpepper, Daunte—Juvenile literature. 2. Football players—United States—Biography—Juvenile literature. [1. Culpepper, Daunte. 2. Football players. 3. African Americans—Biography.] I. Title: Daunte Culpepper. II. Title. III. Series.
   GV939.C82 T56 2003
   796.332'092—dc21

                                                 2002005607

Printed in the United States of America

10 9 8 7 6 5 4 3 2 1

To Our Readers:
We have done our best to make sure all Internet Addresses in this book were active and appropriate when we went to press. However, the author and the publisher have no control over and assume no liability for the material available on those Internet sites or on other Web sites they may link to. Any comments or suggestions can be sent by e-mail to comments@enslow.com or to the address on the back cover.

Photo Credits: © Mark Brettingen/NFL Photos, pp. 6, 21, 29, 32, 41; © Greg Crisp/NFL Photos, pp. 8, 15, 40; © Garrett Ellwood/NFL Photos, pp. 10, 25; © Allen Kee/NFL Photos, pp. 23, 35; © Rick Kolodziej/NFL Photos, p. 39; © NFLP/Al Messerschmidt/NFL Photos, p. 27; © Marty Morrow/NFL Photos, p. 30; © J. C. Ridley/NFL Photos, p. 34; © Joe Robbins/NFL Photos, pp. 1, 4, 12, 17, 19, 37; © David Stluka/NFL Photos, p. 44.

Cover Photo: © Joe Robbins/NFL Photos.

CONTENTS

Introduction

Daunte Culpepper is a quarterback for the Minnesota Vikings. Culpepper can pass the ball well. But what makes him an even more dangerous player is that he is also an excellent runner. Opposing teams do not know if Culpepper is going to pass the ball or run with it. That makes him harder to stop.

Football teams move up the field by running or passing the ball. It is up to players like fullbacks and halfbacks to run with the ball. It is up to quarterbacks to pass the ball. A team's success often depends on how good its quarterback is.

One of the reasons Culpepper runs so well is his size and strength. He is big for a quarterback. He is six feet four inches tall. He weighs 260 pounds and can bench-press more than 400 pounds.

Daunte Culpepper is great at passing and running with the ball.

"That's kind of scary when the quarterback weighs more than you," said Mike Rucker, a defensive end for the Carolina Panthers.

"The guy is like a fullback," said Sam Rogers, a linebacker for the Buffalo Bills. "You have to make sure you get your head across his body when you try to tackle him. You can't come from the back side and expect to blow him up, because you'll bounce right off."

Culpepper is fast. He can run the 40-yard dash in 4.6 seconds. That is a terrific time. As a passer, he can throw the ball 80 yards. That is almost the entire length of a football field.

On top of all that, he is smart. His former coach, Dennis Green, says, "One of his strengths is poise and his ability to make good decisions."

Culpepper has all the valuable skills for a football player. With him running the show, the Vikings are a tough team to beat.

CHAPTER 1

Getting Off on the Right Foot

The spotlight was on Daunte Culpepper. It was the first game of the 2000 season. Culpepper was starting at quarterback for the Minnesota Vikings.

The year before, the Vikings had picked Culpepper in the National Football League (NFL) draft. The draft is the way NFL teams pick new players each year. The Vikings used their first pick to select Culpepper. Minnesota passed up the chance to take other good players.

Culpepper barely played his first season. He spent the year learning. By the next season, Coach Dennis Green thought Culpepper was ready to lead the Vikings. Others were not so sure. Even some of his teammates wondered if he was ready.

The Vikings had big hopes for the 2000 season. But they would have a rookie quarterback leading them. If it did not work out, Green was going to look bad. He was counting on Culpepper to come through.

The Minnesota Vikings picked Daunte Culpepper as their first draft pick in 1999.

Green was not the only person who believed in his new quarterback. Culpepper knew he could do it. He said, "I never doubted myself. Not one time."

The Vikings played the Chicago Bears. The Bears made it hard to complete a pass. They put extra defenders on Randy Moss and Cris Carter, Minnesota's great receivers. On the first play, Culpepper dropped back. His receivers were covered. Unable to pass, Culpepper put his speed to work. He took off and ran for 24 yards. Two plays later, he had another long run.

The Vikings got to the Chicago 26-yard line. This time, Chicago tried something different. Instead of covering the receivers, they put on a big pass rush. The Bears blitzed, sending in more players against Culpepper. There were too many for the Vikings' linemen to block. Bears cornerback Thomas Smith sailed in. He got within a couple steps of Culpepper. Smith thought he was going to sack him. "I had him. He was mine," Smith said later. But Culpepper

Culpepper can throw the ball as well as run with it.

calmly stepped out of the way, and Smith missed him. Other tacklers stormed in, and one got a hold of Culpepper. This time he could not run. Instead, he shoveled the ball ahead to John Davis, his tight end. Davis ran with the ball for a nice gain. It was the first pass Culpepper completed in the NFL.

Culpepper had a good day passing. He completed more than half the passes he attempted. But he did even better with his feet.

The Vikings were behind, 20–9, in the third quarter. Minnesota got close to the goal line. Culpepper kept the ball and carried it in for a one-yard touchdown. That closed the gap, but the Vikings still trailed.

Minnesota started a drive on its own 7-yard line. Culpepper moved his team downfield. He had a big pass to Randy Moss, the Vikings' great receiver. Culpepper finished the drive by keeping the ball again. He ran for a 4-yard touchdown. The Vikings now had the lead. Culpepper made sure they would not lose it.

A few minutes later, he ran the ball for another touchdown.

"Nobody knows when I'm going to run," Culpepper said after the game. "We didn't plan all those runs. It may be that I will, because I want to win. Defenses will make me make decisions like that."

The Vikings won the game against the Bears, 30–27. More importantly, Culpepper proved he could play in the NFL.

His coach agreed. "He's got a lot of confidence in himself," said Green, "and we've got a lot of confidence in him."

UP CLOSE

Daunte Culpepper has thrown 21 of his 47 career touchdown passes to Randy Moss.

A Great Mom

Sometimes when a quarterback gets rushed by defensive players, he finds himself surrounded by people. Culpepper is used to crowds. He comes from a very big family. His mother, Emma Culpepper, raised fourteen children.

All were foster children or children that Emma adopted. Some were her brother's children. Her brother's widow had many more kids. Emma took in seven of them. She then raised some of her children's children. "I had my hands full, but the good Lord and me brought up these kids," Emma said.

When Emma was sixty-two, she thought she was done with raising kids. At the time, she worked at a correctional facility for girls in Ocala, Florida. A sixteen-year-old girl, an inmate, had a baby boy on January 28, 1977. The girl knew she could not care for her new son. She asked Emma for help. Emma did not think she could handle raising another child. But she could not bring herself to turn the girl down. "I finally agreed to take him. I'm so glad I did."

In this way, Daunte became the last child raised by Emma Culpepper. He never knew his mother or father. But, thanks to Emma, he grew up in a good home. "She was loving and caring, but she was also very strict," Culpepper said of his mother. "She was both my mom and my dad."

The family did not have much money, but Emma made sure Daunte got what he needed.

Thanks to Emma Culpepper, Daunte grew up in a good home.

She borrowed a violin, and Daunte learned how to play it. He also played the cello, a larger stringed instrument. "He could play that thing," Emma said. "It was bigger than he was."

Not for long. As Culpepper grew, it became clear he was going to be a good athlete. When he got to middle school, he gave up music lessons and turned to football. One of the reasons it took so long was that Emma could not afford the fee to get him into youth football.

Finally, when he was twelve, Culpepper started his football career. Once he got started, there was no way to stop him.

Standing Out in Sports

Daunte Culpepper went to Vanguard High School in Ocala, Florida. He quickly stood out from the other students. Culpepper played four sports. He was a star in baseball, basketball, weightlifting, and football.

In baseball, he had an offer from a professional team. The New York Yankees drafted him. He did not sign a baseball contract, though. Culpepper wanted to play football.

In basketball, he scored an average of 19.5 points per game. He also averaged 11.3 rebounds per game. He could pass the ball and had a lot of assists. His quickness helped him on defense. He averaged more than three steals per game. A lot of colleges tried to recruit Culpepper to come to their school and play basketball.

In weightlifting, he could already bench-press nearly 350 pounds.

Culpepper played football three years for the Vanguard Knights. He passed for more than 6,000 yards. He had fifty-seven touchdown passes. Both set school records. He was great running the ball, too. He rushed for nearly 1,000 yards and for 26 touchdowns.

He had his best season when he was a senior. He was named Mr. Football by the Florida Athletic Coaches Association. He also earned All-America honors. He was not just the best player in Florida. He was one of the best in the entire country.

Culpepper led Vanguard High School to its first undefeated regular season. The Knights made it all the way to the state championship game. Vanguard played Bradenton Southeast High. Southeast led late in the game. But Culpepper brought the Knights downfield. At one point, Vanguard faced a fourth down and had 20 yards to go. Culpepper went back to pass, but he could not find anyone open. Culpepper scrambled to avoid tacklers, and he

Many colleges wanted him to play basketball, but Culpepper wanted to play football.

took off. He got the first down. Culpepper kept the drive going, but it did not matter. The Knights missed a field goal that could have won the game for them.

Even though Vanguard High came up short, people wanted to know more about Daunte Culpepper.

Many colleges wanted him to come to their school and play football. Even before his big senior season, Culpepper was being recruited. Florida has some major college football programs. University of Miami, University of Florida, and Florida State University all wanted Culpepper to play for them. A smaller school, the University of Central Florida, also recruited him.

It looked like Culpepper would have a lot of choices. Culpepper was a great athlete, but he was not doing as well in the classroom. A player needs a grade point average (GPA) of at least 2.0 (a C average) to play sports in college.

Culpepper had very poor grades when he was a junior. It did not look like he would be able

Culpepper had to work hard in school to be able to play football in college.

to get his GPA up to a 2.0 by the time he graduated. The big schools lost interest in him. They thought he would not make it with his grades.

An assistant coach with Central Florida still had hope. Paul Lounsberry sat down with Culpepper and looked over his classes. They put together a study program.

Culpepper had always worked hard at sports. Now he worked even harder with schoolwork. Finally, he did as well with his grades as he did playing football. He made the honor roll when he was a senior at Vanguard. It meant he would be able to play in college.

The big schools like Miami and Florida State were interested in Culpepper again. But Culpepper did not want to go to those schools. He remembered how Central Florida had stuck with him.

"Central Florida showed they had faith in me," Culpepper said. "They made a commitment to me, so that's where I was going to school."

A Big Stick in College

Daunte Culpepper wanted to do well in school as well as on the football field. Culpepper majored in secondary education at Central Florida.

He was a star on the football field. Culpepper's first game came against Eastern Kentucky. He was nervous, but he studied films of Eastern Kentucky, which had a great team. It paid off.

On Culpepper's first play, he tried to pass. He never got the pass off.

He was sacked. But Culpepper got back up and did well. He completed all five passes he threw as the Central Florida Golden Knights went more than 80 yards for a touchdown. Culpepper changed the play he had planned four times on that drive. When Culpepper saw how the defense lined up, he sometimes thought a different play would work better. He was able to do this because of the time he had spent watching the films of Eastern Kentucky.

Usually, only veteran quarterbacks can do this. For a player to do this in his first college game is amazing.

Culpepper had three touchdown passes in the game. Central Florida beat Eastern Kentucky, 40–32. "Spectacular and extraordinary do not begin to describe it," said Culpepper's coach, Gene McDowell. "My guess is that it was the best first-time performance by any freshman quarterback at any level."

Culpepper played well the entire season. He was happy about how things were working out.

"My first year was everything I could have imagined," he said. "I believe I made the right decision in coming here."

Central Florida was happy, too. Schools like Notre Dame and Florida State play football at the Division I–A level, the top level. The Golden Knights played at the Division I–AA level, but they wanted to move up to the higher level.

Thanks to Culpepper, they were able to do that. Central Florida started playing in Division I-A in 1996. The Golden Knights played better teams, so they did not win as

Daunte Culpepper is about to throw the ball.

many games. But Culpepper showed he could play with and against the best.

In 1997, Central Florida played University of Nebraska. Nebraska was one of the top teams in the country. Nebraska won the game, 38–24. Even though his team lost, Culpepper was fantastic. He passed for more than 300 yards. He also did some great running. Culpepper carried the ball for a 10-yard touchdown. He fought off Nebraska tacklers on his way into the end zone.

Central Florida has an award called the Big Stick. It goes to the player with the biggest hit in each game. A quarterback usually is not known for making big hits. But Culpepper did some hard hitting on his touchdown run. He won the Big Stick Award for the game against Nebraska.

Culpepper was hitting the books hard, too. He made the honor roll when he was a junior. He also got the school's award for football on National Student-Athlete Day.

During his college football career, Culpepper played like a veteran quarterback.

As a senior, everything went well for Culpepper and his team. Central Florida won nine games and lost only two. It was their first winning season since moving up to the top level in college football.

Culpepper was the reason the Golden Knights did so well. He completed 73.6% of his passes. That set a new college record. Fifteen years earlier, Steve Young set that record at Brigham Young University. He then went on to a great career in the NFL.

Culpepper won the 1998 Sammy Baugh Trophy as the college

After a great college football career, Daunte Culpepper was ready for the NFL.

passer of the year. Some outstanding quarterbacks, such as Young and John Elway, had won the Baugh Trophy in the past. Culpepper also finished sixth in the voting for the Heisman Trophy. The Heisman Trophy goes to the best college football player each year.

When Culpepper was in high school, a lot of college recruiters came to watch him. Now he was being watched by the pro teams.

★★ ★ **UP CLOSE**

Daunte Culpepper has set many team records. During the 2000 season, Culpepper threw for over three touchdowns in seven games.

CHAPTER 5 Waiting His Turn

Every year, the National Football League (NFL) holds a draft. Each team takes turns picking college players. In 1999, the Minnesota Vikings had the eleventh pick in the draft. Their coach, Dennis Green, was excited about Culpepper. However, the Vikings already had some good quarterbacks. Culpepper would not get a chance to play right away with the Vikings.

Some people thought the Vikings should take a player who could help them immediately. One of the players available was Jevon Kearse, a defensive lineman. However, Green insisted that the Vikings take Culpepper. Kearse was drafted by the Tennessee Titans. He had a great first season and helped the Titans get to the Super Bowl.

Green took a lot of heat for not taking Kearse. Maybe the Vikings could have made it to the Super Bowl if they had taken him. But Green was sure he had made a good decision with Culpepper.

In 1999, Culpepper got some playing time in the preseason games. He did not impress anyone in those games. He seemed unsure of himself, he made bad passes, and he got sacked a lot.

During the regular season, Culpepper practiced with the Vikings. But he played only one game. And in that game, he did not even throw a pass.

But Dennis Green had plans for Culpepper.

The Vikings had outstanding receivers. Randy Moss, one of them, may be the best receiver in football. Green looked forward to the day when Culpepper would be

In 1999, Culpepper played only one game.

34

Culpepper knew he could help the Vikings win.

firing passes to Moss. That would be an unbeatable combination, he thought.

Randall Cunningham and Jeff George were the quarterbacks for the Vikings in 1999. The team did not keep either one of them for the 2000 season. Minnesota tried to get a veteran quarterback. Dan Marino was one of the quarterbacks they thought about signing. But that did not work out.

In April 2000, Green announced that Culpepper would lead the Vikings in 2000. "We're always trying to win," he explained, "and so every decision we make is based on what we think is going to help us win. It's not based on anything other than that. We want to win."

Culpepper knew he could help the Vikings win. He certainly did in the first game of the season when he ran for three touchdowns against the Chicago Bears.

And he kept the Vikings going. It was a long time before the team lost with Culpepper in charge.

Getting His Chance

Daunte Culpepper threw his first touchdown pass in the second game of the season. It was a 15-yard pass to Moss. The Vikings beat the Miami Dolphins, 13–7. In that game, Culpepper passed for more than 350 yards. The Vikings kept rolling. Culpepper had two touchdown passes in a win against the New England Patriots. The next week, he added three more touchdown passes, all to Moss, as Minnesota beat the Detroit Lions.

The Vikings won all their games in September. They kept rolling in October. Minnesota played the Tampa Bay Buccaneers in a Monday night game on national television. Culpepper started the scoring by running for a 27-yard touchdown. The Vikings trailed in the fourth quarter. Culpepper then connected with Moss for a 42-yard touchdown. The Vikings won the game.

Minnesota won its first seven games of the season before finally losing. The Vikings went on to win the Central Division title. Their first

In 2000, Daunte Culpepper and the Vikings went to the NFC championship game.

playoff game was against New Orleans. Culpepper had a great game. He connected with Randy Moss for two touchdowns. One was for 53 yards and the other for 68 yards. Culpepper also hooked up with Cris Carter on a 17-yard touchdown. Culpepper finished the game with more than 300 yards passing. The Vikings won easily and went to the National Football Conference (NFC) championship game. If they won, they would go to the Super Bowl. Unfortunately, the Vikings lost to the New York Giants in the NFC championship game.

Daunte Culpepper is active in his community.

Culpepper does great things on the field and off.

Culpepper's season was not over. He was named the starting quarterback for the NFC in the Pro Bowl, the league's All-Star game. It was a great honor, and it was because Culpepper had a great season. He passed for nearly 4,000 yards and had 33 touchdown passes. He also ran the ball for 470 yards. He averaged more than five yards per carry.

Culpepper has come a long way in his life. But he has never forgotten where he started. After he went to the NFL, he remembered his mom. He surprised Emma with a new home.

Culpepper is also involved in community activities. When he was in college, he worked with a program known as Bright Knights, which teaches young students the importance of education. He was in another program to provide positive role models to disadvantaged youth.

Today, Culpepper still gives back. He is active with an African-American adoption agency. Because of adoption, Culpepper grew up in a good home. He wants others to have good homes, too.

This is all a part of who Daunte Culpepper is. He is an exciting and great football player. But he is an even greater person.

UP CLOSE

Daunte Culpepper holds a Viking record of 27 games in a row with over 100 yards passing.

CAREER STATISTICS

NFL									
Passing									
Year	Team	GP	Comp.	Att.	Yds.	Pct.	TDs	Int.	Rating
1999	Minnesota	1	0	0	0	0.0	0	0	0.0
2000	Minnesota	16	297	474	3,937	62.7	33	16	98.0
2001	Minnesota	11	235	366	2,612	64.2	14	13	83.3
Totals		28	532	840	6,549	63.3	47	29	91.6

Rushing						
Year	Team	GP	Att.	Yds.	Avg.	TDs
1999	Minnesota	1	3	6	2.0	0
2000	Minnesota	16	89	470	5.3	7
2001	Minnesota	11	71	416	5.9	5
Totals		28	163	892	5.5	12

GP—Games Played
Att.—Attempts
Comp.—Passes Completed

Pct.—Percentage of Passes
    Completed
Yds.—Yards Gained

TD—Touchdowns
Int.—Interceptions

Where to Write to Daunte Culpepper

Mr. Daunte Culpepper
c/o Minnesota Vikings
9520 Viking Drive
Eden Prairie, Minnesota 55344

Daunte Culpepper is a good football player and role model.

WORDS TO KNOW

cornerback—A defensive back. It is his job to cover receivers.

draft—A selection of players by teams, who take turns choosing the players they want.

Heisman Trophy—The award that is given each year to the best college football player in America.

junior—An eleventh-grade student in high school or a third-year student in college.

quarterback—He is in charge of the offense. He calls the plays, sometimes with help from the bench. The quarterback can either pass the ball, hand it off to a running back, or keep it and run.

rookie—A player in his first full season in professional sports.

sack—To tackle a quarterback attempting to pass the ball behind the line of scrimmage.

senior—A twelfth-grade student in high school or a fourth-year student in college.

tight end—Usually a big player who catches passes and blocks for runners.

READING ABOUT

Minnesota Vikings Staff. *Minnesota Vikings*. White Plains, N.Y.: Everett Sports Publishing and Marketing, 1998.

Nelson, Julie. *Minnesota Vikings*. Mankato, Minn.: The Creative Company, 2000.

Stewart, Mark. *Daunte Culpepper: Command and Control.* Brookfield, Conn.: Millbrook Press, 2002.

Internet Addresses

Daunte Culpepper on The Sporting News Web site
<http://www.sportingnews.com/nfl/players/4659/stats.html>

The Official Web Site of the Vikings
<http://www.vikings.com/>

INDEX